The Two Lives Of Shirley Mae

Larry George Pickett

ISBN: 978-1-989506-67-7
Copyright © 2023 Larry George Pickett

Published in Canada by Pandamonium Publishing House™
www.pandamoniumpublishing.com
pandapublishing8@gmail.com

DEDICATION

To my little sister, Shirley Mae, who waits with our parents, Vernon and Laura and big sister Diane to finish our story.

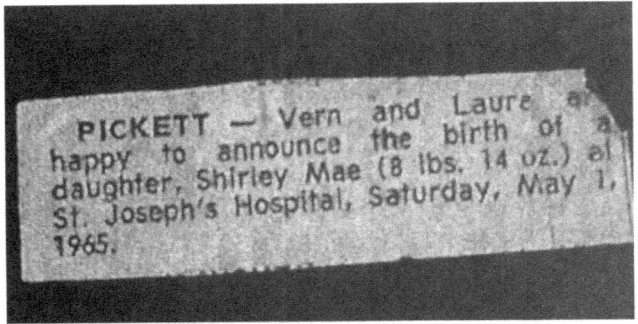

PICKETT — Vern and Laura are happy to announce the birth of a daughter, Shirley Mae (8 lbs. 14 oz.) at St. Joseph's Hospital, Saturday, May 1, 1965.

THE TWO LIVES OF SHIRLEY MAE

CONTENTS

1

There are thousands of stories of past events that many people accept as fact even though there is no physical evidence that these events ever happened. Did Moses reach out with his staff and part the Red sea? Did Muhammad actually split the moon in half? Did Jesus of Nazareth heal the sick by simply laying hands upon them and did he walk on water? Many write these stories off as fables and fantasy but there are and have been billions who truly believe them. So much so that they base their entire lives and even their afterlives on them being true.

They say that they believe them because of their faith which was defined once as, *the assurance of things hoped for and the conviction of things unseen.* I wonder how many small inexplicable events have happened that have never been documented and therefore have been forgotten with the passing of time. How many billions of non-earth-shattering stories with no physical evidence to support ever happening, actually have. Such is the case with my little sister Shirley Mae.

It began in the mid-fifties when the oldest baby boomers were just starting to hit double digits, age wise. Even so, their influence could already be seen on both large and small screens with television sets rapidly replacing radios in every home. Disney became a household word and businesses were bending over backwards to create all things child pleasing. It was a great time to be a kid.

I was in the sweet spot of this wave and the youngest of seven children. Our neighborhood was working middle-class but being renters rather than owners of our home we would have been considered somewhere below that standing. I never felt that, though, and in fact I virtuously never sensed any want. Seven children and two adults living in a one washroom, three-bedroom home I'm sure presented challenges, but our childhoods were happy for the most part.

My three brothers, Gord, Mark, and David and my three sisters, Carolynn, Diane, and Linda supplied me with endless excitement, drama, and laughter. My parents were both hard workers partly because of necessity but mostly because it was their nature. All together we were a close family which helped a great deal when Shirley Mae came into our lives. Even though I was barely five years old when she arrived, I still remember all the time I spent with her, especially the first day. It was four days after my birthday, in fact, Shirley Mae was born on my fifth birthday, July 26th, 1956. I was warned that since she was only a few days old and fragile I needed to be careful with her. This could not have been further from the truth. The very first time I looked into her eyes she met my gaze with the strength of a tiger. I felt she was telling me something with that look. It was an all-knowing look that only comes from extreme confidence.

Perhaps it was just my imagination but as she reached out her tiny hand beckoning me it seemed as if she was inviting me to join her in some amazing adventure, she had already decided would be her life. I reached out and she gripped my baby finger so tightly that I could tell she was extraordinarily strong, and I could see she was not fragile at all but was ready for anything the world could throw at her. It was exciting to believe she was asking me to join her in her grand adventure. Each day I would watch her, and she would smile to let me know that the plan was all set, and I need only be a little patient and it would unfold.

It was two weeks to the day from when my mom and dad had brought Shirley Mae home when I came into our living room where she stayed in her basket. My mother seemed upset and told me that I could not visit with my little sister today because she wasn't feeling well, and she refused to eat anything. I knew this was strange because I often requested to give my sister her bottle and she would always finish it. I did recall, however, her falling asleep before finishing the day before. I didn't give it any more thought, but I was disappointed to not have my time with her and her usual assurance that all is well with our adventure plans.

2

2

Later that day I was at my friend Jim's house who lived next door to us when his mother surprised me by telling me that my father had called on the phone and needed me to come home now. It wasn't near supper time, and I didn't remember doing anything wrong so I had no idea why he would want me home.

I came in through the front door and entered our living room. Most of my brothers and sisters were there looking upset and my father was hugging my mom who was crying. I didn't see Shirley Mae in her basket and before I could ask where she was my mom spoke through her tears and simply said, "She's gone, Larry".

I didn't know what she meant. My first thought was that somehow my little sister had decided to start her great adventure and I would have to catch up with her when ready.

I asked, "Where did she go?"

But my father only replied, "She's gone to a better place".

That didn't help me at all. I had no idea where he meant, and I sure couldn't guess where she had gone after all I didn't even know where she came from.

In the next few days other clues to her whereabouts were uttered by family members. The word Heaven came up a few times and I heard "she is with the angels" once. It wasn't long until I figured out that wherever she went it was very unlikely that I would be able to catch up with her and I accepted that her decision to leave me behind was made with my safety in mind.

I was a little confused, however, why everyone was unhappy when they all believed she was in "a better place". I guess I was a little sad to be left behind, but I was happy for Shirley Mae to be able to go on her great adventure so early. I started to imagine the new life she would have and decided to tell everyone in my life about it.

3

I had virtually forgotten my arrival into this world by the time my mom brought me home. Just flashes of a cold bright room with three masked people in white moving me about and a vague resentment of being forced from the warm safe place that I never wanted to leave. Only after being wrapped warmly and placed in my mother's arms were my memories clear. I could remember the love shining from her face and the return of that safe feeling I feared had been lost forever. That memory I would never forget.

A quick few days of poking and prodding and I was on my way home as the youngest of 8 children. My three older sisters immediately pleaded to hold me and were given the chance once they sat down as instructed. Although I did not appreciate being awkwardly passed from one to another, I could see the affection in each of their faces and smiled. The smile of course evoked many excited squeals from all. My three oldest brothers declined the chance to hold me even before it was offered to them. This was to be expected but Larry, my youngest brother, couldn't wait for a chance. I'm not sure why he was so drawn to me. Perhaps it was that he was the closest to me in age or possibly it was because, after five long years, he was no longer the baby of the family and felt he owed me a great debt for taking over that undesirable position.

Our connection was instant and the bond, although non-verbal, was undeniable. Everyone could see it. Because it was so obvious, he was given special privileges. He was allowed to hold me despite his young age as well as feed me my bottle. It was over those few days that I realized how special our connection was and I shared my plans of adventure.

On the last day Larry fed me I did not make our normal eye contact but looked past him at someone who was standing over his left shoulder. It was a man, looking down at me. Somehow, I knew who he was and was even expecting him. I also knew why he was there. He was to explain to me the details of what was to come. There was no fear but only comfort and joy in his words and in his face, peace.

"You will be leaving tomorrow, Shirley Mae. To prepare for your journey you should stop eating and drinking." He did not move his mouth and yet I could hear and understand him clearly.

"I know I must go but can you tell me why?" I responded, in the same manner as he.

"Why is the last mystery that will be revealed to us when it is time but rest assured that it is all part of the great plan, we are all part of. Your part, Shirley Mae, is not here but in a different place for a different purpose, however, I can tell you this, it will be filled with love, purpose, and fulfillment."

"Would it be possible for my big brother, Larry, to join me in this new place? We have formed a bond between us, and I believe that he wants to come with me."

"It's true that the bond is extraordinary between you. A rare connection that can sometimes happen. It is another mystery and there is certainly a reason for it, but I am sorry he cannot go with you. It is also true that he senses your wish for him to join you, but he believes it is in this place and not in another. His place is here but he will not forget you and your bond will give him insight into your future."

"If I am going by myself, how will I travel? I am too young to even walk by myself."

"You will start your new life at the same age as your brother's, five. This will probably make the bond between you even greater. I can tell you one thing, Shirley Mae, you will absolutely see Larry again."

4

Even at my young age I knew babies as young as Shirley Mae had a definite mobility problem but that did not stop me. It was obvious to see that Shirley Mae was no average child and I knew that there was no telling what she could do. So, there it was. It became so clear to me. She had simply grown bored with the constant poking, toe pulling and silly face making of the endless parade of adults that presented themselves and through sheer willpower had left this place. A very childish idea even for a five-year-old but once I had assumed this, it was easy for me to dream up many adventures that my little sister would enjoy and tell them to all my family and friends.

And so, it was for the next five years but with each passing year my stories seemed less possible to me, and listeners became less receptive, even dismissive at times. I was starting to grow up and as my own faith began to wane, I started to forget my little sister's face. That is until my 10th birthday.

As fortune would have it, there was a carnival in town that day and my parents agreed to take me. It was very crowded with noises of all kinds creating its own excitement. All my brothers and sisters had come as well and were instructed to stay together. We formed a rather large group and even though it was my birthday I quickly blended into the mix. I was having a great day with all my family and remember it was one of the few times that Shirley Mae was totally out of my mind. My brothers and sisters were overexcited, rushing from one ride to another and I fell a few steps behind. As we passed by a small tent with a sign outside reading, "Fortunes Told / Crystal ball, Palms and Tea Leaves", a woman beckoned to me as she did others who were within ear shot.

"Come and learn your future" she cried, and it was enough to slow me another few steps behind the others and I took two steps toward her tent.

That is when I heard it. Somehow a voice broke through all other voices even the fortune tellers and rose over the music and screaming of the giant rides surrounding us. It wasn't special in any other way, but the words grabbed my attention, and I turned around to see their source even as they echoed in my ears.

"Shirley Mae where are you going?" was the phrase and I suppose it was only the first two words that were my focus. The source was a girl who called to another girl who stood between us. The closer girl did not respond but stared silently at me and I sensed something familiar about her and I took a step toward her straining to see her clearly. She suddenly smiled as if discovering a great and good thing. She stepped quickly toward me, and my heart jumped as I recognized her despite her appearing so different.

She came within a step of me and said, "Hey big brother, I'm sorry you couldn't come with me."

As she spoke all other sounds stopped and as I stared into the pair of tiger eyes that I remembered so well, everybody else and everything disappeared, even the girl who called her name. I tried to speak but my shock was so great that nothing would come out of my mouth.

She smiled, stepped to me and as she embraced me whispered in my ear, "Yes, it's me and I am having a good life. I don't know how my being here with you is possible but somehow, I'm sure that I can't stay and that you can't come with me. I want you to know that you are still my big brother and always will be. Thank you for telling the stories about my life. I don't know how you know about me but somehow you do. I know your memory of me is fading but if you keep telling my stories then I'll never be forgotten." She took a step back and continued, "Take a good look at me, big brother, so you won't forget. I will see you again, I'm sure, but I don't know when. I love you, Larry."

As she stood there, I burned her image into my mind, I tried desperately to speak the words I had in my mouth but could not force them out. It was her for certain but grown to match my ten years. The confidence and intellect were still in those tiger eyes and as I tried to lunge toward my baby sister to embrace her, I felt a strong arm grip my shoulder and jerk me hard.

As my gaze was ripped from Shirley Mae the words screamed from my lips, "I love you, Shirley Mae."

After the words were out, I realized that I was now staring at my father who had a worried look on his face. As he began to speak, I quickly turned back in search of my sister, but she was no longer there, and the sounds of the carnival were again deafening. I tried to pull myself free of my father's grip and intended to go running and look for her, but he was too strong. Only after surrendering to my father's will did, I finally hear his words of concern.

"Are you okay, Larry? You seemed to be in another world, son. Why did you call out Shirley Mae's name?"

I only then felt the tears running down my face and my father hugged me believing I was upset and sad, but this was not the case. The tears were of absolute joy from seeing my little sister and knowing that she was having a good life and somehow my imaginings and stories about her were true.

As he held me, I said, "I saw her, dad."

He stepped back but still held my arms and stared at me in disbelief while uttering a single word, "What?"

"She spoke to me too, dad."

The words came out garbled as my emotions overwhelmed me, but he could understand. He gave me a quick hug, turned me and with one arm around my shoulder started to guide me toward the parking lot and our car.

Apparently, my family had moved only a few steps up the midway while I was having my visit with my little sister but, with all the distractions and noise, it was far enough for them to be unaware of my falling behind. My father had been the first to notice.

Now my mother called out, surprised we were heading away from them, and my father called back, "We will catch up. We are going to take a minute."

This didn't stop her, and she quickened her pace to us, but my father again reassured her saying, "It's OK. There's nothing wrong."

It always seemed odd to me that when one parent tried to reassure the other it usually had the opposite effect. This was evident again by the panicked look on my mom's face and the fear in her voice when she said, "Where are you going? What's wrong?"

"Just to the car," he replied, "Larry is just a little upset".

"No mom, I'm not upset. I saw Shirley Mae and she spoke to me."

That's when they exchanged glances at each other and after a moment my mom said, "Go, I'll catch up. I'll tell Gord and Carolynn to watch the others for a few minutes."

"Tell them to stay together and no rides until we get back," my father cautioned unnecessarily.

She was back with us in under a minute, but no one spoke again until we were all in the station wagon. Even then there was silence for a few minutes except for a few whispers between my parents that I could not hear.

Finally, my father spoke in a soft consoling voice, "You know, Larry, your mom and I remember how much you loved your baby sister and when Shirley Mae left us you did not cry or even seem sad. Sometimes when we don't accept that someone is gone it can have a confusing effect on us and sometimes when we miss someone and wish we could be with them again, well, that happens but only in our minds. You know that Shirley Mae wasn't really here, don't you?"

I really didn't know what to say. There was no doubt in my mind that I had been with her and that she had spoken to me. I had no idea why they were not overjoyed.

After a few moments and in a calm and rational voice I replied, "Sorry dad, but you're wrong. It was her. She spoke to me, and she knew my name. She told me that she was living a good life and that she was sorry I could not come along."

"I know, Larry, but…" were the last words my dad spoke in the car. My mom stopped him by reaching out and putting her hand on his shoulder. She spoke in a soft voice. She could not hold back her question any longer.

"What did she look like, Larry?"

She wasn't upset, and although there was a tear in the corner of her eye threatening to escape down her cheek, she was smiling. Her question didn't come from a place of doubt but rather from an absolute need to know.

I smiled when I saw the belief in her eyes but looked at my father for a moment before answering. He understood my silent question, closed his eyes, sighed, and nodded his head in acquiescence.

"She's my age, mom. I don't know how she did it but she's ten years old. She looks different but the same person is still in her face, especially her eyes. You know, the tiger eyes. Her hair is still bright blonde, and she still smiles with her whole face."

As the words poured from me and I began to mentally relive Shirley Mae's visit I could feel my emotions rising again. My eyes were welling up and I struggled to keep control. I needed to tell her all of it.

With a voice a full octave higher, I managed to sneak out, "She hugged me, mom." And after a moment, "She said she loved me."

At this my mother broke down and opened her car door. I wondered where she was going and was immediately shown when she opened my door. She pushed in beside me and hugged me. My father got out without saying anything. He stepped toward the back of the car and lit a cigarette. With my head turned toward the front seat I could see him in the rear-view mirror. I believe he was crying as well but being a man of his generation, he would not let himself be seen breaking down.

After what seemed like a long time and I was back in control of my emotions, I said to her, "It's OK, mom. She's happy. She said she didn't know how I knew but all the stories that I've been telling everyone about her are true. She wants me to write them down so she will never be forgotten and that's what I'm going to do."

She finally leaned back from me, and I could see she had stopped crying and had a look of absolute peace. Somehow something was fixed inside my mother that had been broken for the last five years.

She kissed my cheek and then said," Yes Larry, you must do that. No matter what else you do in your life you must do that." She turned from me and opened the door and stepped out. I could hear her ask my dad if he was ready to go back and join the other kids and I saw him nod in the mirror as he threw down his butt and crushed it with his foot.

As we walked back to the carnival there was a noticeable change in them both. It was a new joy. My parents laughed as if a great burden had been lifted from both of them. When we joined the others, my dad explained to them that I had experienced something that neither he nor our mother could explain. He told them it was something special and that I will share it with them individually in my own time. We had a great time at the carnival that day. It was my best birthday ever.

5

Ocean spray woke me, and I found myself in total darkness. I could taste and feel the frigid salt water I was in but had no memory of where I was, how I got there or even who I was. A flash of lightning lit the sky for a moment, time enough to reveal a dense fog. Even the bright orange life jacket that kept me from slipping below the water could not be seen after the flash had ended. Terror rose inside me as I bobbed helplessly. I screamed out in anguish sensing there was no hope. Then a noise came from behind me. It was almost certainly a voice, but the words were too faint to discern.

I clumsily tried to turn with little success as I screamed through my tears and into the darkness, "Help, I'm here!"

For an eternity no response came to my pitiful cry but then another lightning flash lit the night, and I heard the voice clearly, "We see you. We are coming."

A bright light came from behind and I managed to turn but had to cover my eyes and could not see my rescuers. A woman's voice shouted and pierced the night, almost screaming.

"It's her! I know it is!"

"Stay seated, ma'am, we've got her, " came a calmer response.

Suddenly, I could feel a hand grabbing my jacket and then another. I glimpsed two men as they hauled me up into the bow of a boat and wrapped me in a blanket. With the light finally directed elsewhere I lowered my hands from my face, and I could see others, although poorly, all tightly seated together except one. A woman was standing near the back of the boat and moving toward me, squinting for all she was worth. When she spoke, I recognized the voice as the one that cried out moments before.

"Shirley Mae?"

"Sit down, ma'am! It's not safe," yelled a sailor as he grabbed at her arm, but she would not be stopped.

"No, I must get to her", she screamed as she pulled free, almost losing her balance, and causing the boat to tip slightly.

Another sailor caught her and steadied her then pleaded in a soft voice, "Please stop, ma'am. We will get her to you, but we must move slowly, or the boat may capsize."

Perhaps realizing her folly, the woman conceded to sit but could not wait silently and she called to me, "Shirley Mae is that you?"

It was obvious that she believed I was the one she sought but since I had no idea who I was I could only sit, shivering in silence.

Suddenly the bright light that found me in the sea was trained on the frantic woman and the sailor controlling it asked, "Look child, is that your mother?"

I looked at the woman as she forced herself to keep her eyes open despite the light and I tried to call up even a semblance of a memory but there was none. After a while I said, "I don't know."

A moment later he told me to close my eyes and once they were closed, I could sense the light on my face as my hair was brushed back.

"Can you see her clearly now, ma'am?"

"Yes, it's her. I'm sure." The woman called back and began to rise again but was quickly dissuaded.

"We will move her back to you shortly, but she seems to be in shock, and we should give her a bit before we do that. Just sit tight and we will get her to you soon."

His words filled me with hope that I would eventually regain my memory but as the sun started to rise hours later illuminating our surroundings it added no light to my mind. It was, however, deemed safer in the daylight to slowly move me back to my would-be mother.

The memory of my life before that day never returned. I accepted without question the details of it relayed to me by the lady who comforted me so lovingly. She told me that my name was Shirley Mae, I was five years old to the day and now, a survivor of the Andrea Doria shipwreck that claimed fifty-one lives. My family was apparently quite well off, but I was an only child. We lived in New York City, and I attended an all-girl private school. Peggy Sue, my best friend who was way ahead on the maturity level, always talked about boys and how we were being seriously damaged socially by not having any at our school. She tended to talk constantly about whatever happened to come into her mind, but I was comfortable with her, and we seemed to be a natural fit, with me being the quiet one.

For the next year, my life was good with friends and family but there always seemed to be a mystery about the time before my rescue.

On the night of my sixth birthday I had, what seemed to be, at the time, a bizarre dream that was more like a memory from that missing time. It became a recurring one and always began the same way. A boy that seemed familiar to me was looking down at me, smiling, talking to me about a great adventure we would be going on. I could see that he loved me, and I sensed an almost telepathic bond between us. He spoke with excitement in his voice and in his eyes and called me by my name. At first the dream disturbed me, almost frightening me but gradually I felt myself drawing closer to him. Soon I found myself looking forward to our nightly visits.

I confided in Peggy Sue who Immediately blamed our sorry boy-less environment. I explained that my feeling for the boy was not of that nature but rather like he was my brother. She then suggested that I was dreaming up a sibling because, being an only child, I craved one. I resented this notion but had to admit the possibility. Each night the dream was the same until my seventh birthday.

On that night the dream changed completely except for the little boy. He was there but he sat and spoke to a group of people of different ages. They called him Larry and it rang true when I heard it as if I had known it all along. They all seemed enthralled by his story, and I strained to hear his words. I was shocked into consciousness upon hearing the first line that he spoke.

"Ocean spray awoke her, and she found herself in total darkness," he said.

How could he know something that happened to me two years past? I asked myself. *Surely it is just me putting words into his mouth from my own memories.* When I told my mother about my dream, the mention of the day I was almost lost upset her so much that I decided to keep my dreams to myself in the future. There didn't seem to be anything she could do to help anyway.

I asked Peggy Sue and she agreed with me, which gave me a small bit of assurance. *Yes, this must be it,* I told myself, but that theory was quickly discredited as each night he continued my life story and added details I didn't know myself. He described my father's occupation as a bank executive and how it took up most of his time which left little for me or my mother. I was sure that I did not know my fathers' precise occupation myself but still I reasoned that perhaps I had heard it mentioned in the past but kept the fact only in my subconscious.

With each passing night he would continue, and I could slowly piece together much of who he was. I learned about his family and his place in it. I could deduce through remarks from the others in the dream that they were brothers and sisters, seven siblings in all. The dreams continued each night for a year with the stories slowly moving forward toward my present day.

6

On my 8th birthday there was another startling revelation. It came in the form of a question posed by one of the older brothers and for the first time showed my possible connection to them all.

With a voice filled with resentment he interrupted his brother asking, "Why do you think that our little sister, Shirley Mae, is living this other life and even if she is, how could you possibly know?"

As the immensity of his words sank in, I was suddenly afraid but did not wake. *Why would he speak as if I were with them at one time?* I asked myself. Then I thought of the missing part of my life and grew even more afraid but then came the reply that washed over me like sunshine and removed all my apprehension.

"I don't know how or why I know but somehow I do, and I will tell my stories so that our little sister, who we all love, will live on even if it is not with us and so she will never be forgotten."

Even though the question seemed designed to hurt Larry, his answer was meant to edify and held nothing but assurance. So much so that his brother was completely disarmed and seemed regretful as he silently sat down.

Larry continued his stories, and they were accurate in every detail, but they also had even more meaning to me. I listened as his sister now and felt the connection growing much stronger. He was now only a short time behind my present day.

What would happen then? I asked myself. Perhaps the dreams would stop or maybe Larry would start creating fictional stories. The answer came on my 9th birthday.

That night the dream changed again, and I thought my guess was true. He told a story about my father being transferred and that meant we would have to move to Toronto, Canada. *Finally*, I thought, *a story that couldn't possibly be true. Perhaps the dreams will finally stop.*

That morning at the breakfast table both my mother and father were there. A rarity but it was only a hint of what was to come. Apparently, my father's bank was going international, and he was offered a vice presidency at a new branch. Needless to say, it was in Toronto, Canada. We were to move in three months.

Peggy Sue was devastated but I assured her that my new home was not that far away, and we would be able to see each other again. This of course was very unlikely, or so I thought. We kept in touch with a few letters and an occasional phone call, but they became fewer and fewer until there were virtually none.

The dreams continued without any more revelations about my future. In fact, the dreams became intermittent, and the settings were now changing. It seemed as though they were now a window into my brother's life, and I quickly became an eager spectator. The few stories that were told, however, became almost routine and it seemed that Larry was losing interest in telling them. He too was growing up and I wondered if perhaps he was dismissing my existence as a childish fantasy. Maybe he was forgetting me altogether. I was saddened by these possibilities because I had started to believe that somehow everything was true. That I was their little sister.

7

A week before my 10th birthday my parents surprised me. It was considered a significant milestone and they wanted to make it special. They had made arrangements for Peggy Sue to come all the way from New York to spend a week with me and to celebrate with us. There was to be another surprise on my special day, but they would not give me even a hint.

Peggy Sue arrived right on time, a few days before my big day. I wasn't going to tell her about the progression of my dreams, but she asked the first time we were alone. She was so intrigued that she managed to sit quietly while I caught her up. Maybe she had grown up a bit too.

After she arrived I had a radically different experience as I dreamt. I seemed to be more than a spectator but not really there either. I was somewhere in between. I could walk freely and move about at will. They were at a carnival and as they spoke it became clear they were celebrating Larry's 10th birthday.

Each night I could see them arriving there. They were all having a great time going on rides and playing games. The dream was the same until the eve of my birthday. At first, there was no difference, and I was almost complacent even enjoying my dream but something different occurred. As I watched the family group, Larry began to fall behind the others. He was distracted by someone shouting from his right. It was a woman calling to the crowd.

"Come and learn your future."

He stopped for a moment and became enthralled by her. He took two steps toward her tent. Seeing his interest, she spoke to him directly saying, "Do you have questions about your future, little man?"

"Not about my future", he replied," but can you tell me about my little sister and *her* future? Can you tell me if she remembers me and if I will ever see her again?"

I was suddenly afraid. What would be revealed here? A sense of dread filled me, and I drew closer to Larry as she replied.

"The leaves tell all and the ball sees all. Come into my tent and all will be revealed."

He glanced toward his family who were still only a few steps away, obviously weighing the possible harm of falling behind against the chance to know if his stories were really true. It proved to be too hard to resist as he replied.

"I only have a dollar and two minutes. Is that enough time?" he asked.

"Yes, it is enough." She took his arm and his money, threw open the flap of her tent and ushered him inside. I followed, unobserved, and stood over them after they sat down.

The act was typically predictable with the woman waving her hands over a ball that sat between them, eyes closed and moaning.

"I am in touch with the spirit world now," she declared after a few short moments then continued, "ask your questions and all will be revealed."

"Where is my little sister? Will I see her again?"

Suddenly she opened her eyes and stared deep into the ball and cried out, "It is very cloudy, but I can see that she has traveled a great distance and you will see her again".

"But can you see where she has gone?" Larry asked again with a tinge of desperation in his voice.

"Look into the ball as you call out her name and perhaps the clouds will disperse," she said.

Larry drew near to the ball, his eyes within an inch of it and called out, "Shirley Mae, it's me, your brother." Then after a moment of silence he asked, "Can you hear me, Shirley Mae? Are you on a great adventure?"

The fortune teller broke in now declaring, "Yes, Shirley Mae can hear you and she says she will be coming home soon."

"What do you mean she will be coming home soon?" he asked, obviously surprised.

"That is all that will be revealed, my little friend. Your time is up."

"Do you mean she didn't go to heaven?" Larry demanded.

The woman, realizing her mistake, appeared embarrassed to have been revealed as a fake. She became anxious to finish the session and spoke impatiently, as she stood and moved toward the door.

"This is why the ball was so clouded. It cannot see past the veil of death. I cannot answer questions that are made with lies. Your sister is not on some adventure, and you will not see her again."

Larry looked bewildered. I could see by the look on his face that he was totally shocked and dismayed. He slowly rose from his chair, turned, and walked toward the door. The woman threw open the flap and stared at him as though he had committed some great wrong, as he passed by her. I was only a few steps behind him and as I neared the door, she turned her head back, stopping at me when her expression suddenly changed. Her eyes widened and she screamed in horror. The scream woke me from my sleep, but I could have sworn that somehow, she saw me.

***

In the morning I told Peggy Sue about the strange dream, but she was so excited about it being my big day that she barely listened, dismissing it as another of my endless night dramas. Her excitement about the day, however, helped me to refocus and I quickly became excited as I suddenly remembered the promised surprise to come. We went down to breakfast where my parents were waiting wearing matching smiles. I could smell my favorite breakfast, blueberry pancakes, which was a good start to the day and the surprise was to be revealed after we finished eating. I began to devour my stack anxious to find out what it was.

My father put his hand on my shoulder and said, "Slow down Shirley Mae! OK, obviously you can't wait so we will tell you now. What is the place you've always wanted to go since I can remember?

"Wait, what, are you taking us to a circus? I asked hopefully.

"Well not quite, there are no circuses in the area until the fall, but we did find something pretty close. There just happens to be a carnival opening today and we are all going!"

The word carnival knocked my mind into chaos. It was as if two worlds had instantly collided and somehow, I knew that it was more than some weird coincidence.

The expression on my face was obviously not what they expected and after a moment my mother spoke, "Are you alright Shirl? We thought you would be ecstatic. I'm sorry it couldn't be an actual circus, but this carnival is supposed to be huge with some animal acts, clowns and other circus-like things."

I finally regained order in my mind and returned to the moment. I glanced at Peggy Sue who was a little wide-eyed herself apparently having recalled my mention of a carnival in my dream. I forced myself to smile and reassured my mom.

"Yes, yes of course, I was just so surprised. I had no idea what to expect and this is so great I was just a little overwhelmed, that's all."

"Oh good, that's a relief," she said. "You had us worried for a second. Now eat up. We are leaving shortly after breakfast. It's a couple of hours drive, and we want to be there by noon."

The pace and volume of my pancake consumption decreased so much that it prompted another query, this time from my dad if I was alright. I told him it was just all the excitement which reassured him. As Peggy Sue and I got ready for the day upstairs she reverted to Peggy Sue mode asking questions faster than I could respond.

"Is that weird or what? Do you think there's a connection? It must be just a coincidence; don't you think Shirley?"

"I'm sure it's just a coincidence," I finally responded but only to quiet her. Somehow, I was absolutely sure there was something happening that I didn't understand and probably couldn't be explained by anyone.

***

We arrived exactly on time, which was no surprise with my fathers' meticulous scheduling abilities. Lunch consisted of a hotdog and coke for Peggy Sue and me which we quickly downed, but the adults ordered a full hot meal. Apparently, they had decided to make it a date day for themselves, and we were allowed to go on our own with strict rules and a rendezvous point for exactly two o'clock. It only took a few rides, and we were in full carnival mode, but the dream was always in the back of my mind. After the third roller coaster the hot dogs began to not sit well, and we decided to stroll up the midway and took turns playing games. I won a small doll and Peggy Sue was now trying to match my prize. As she threw baseballs somewhere in the vicinity of bowling pin targets, I allowed my attention to stray from her efforts and took a few steps from her. It's hard to describe the sensation that came over me when I spotted the tent at the end of the line of game booths. It was a strange combination of intrigue and anxiety, but I felt no real fear. There was no doubt in my mind that I was exactly where I was supposed to be, needed to be, in fact. The old woman was there barking to anyone who would listen while most didn't. I listened with my contempt growing as I recalled her treatment of my big brother in my dream. She was the one who destroyed his belief in me and the stories he told. She was just a charlatan with no good in her and had no right to do so much harm.

As I stood there still pondering the situation and all its possibilities a crowd came from my left passing close in front of me then turning away to continue up the midway. As they quickly passed there seemed something familiar about them. First one face then another from the dreams, and although I got only glimpses of profiles, I was sure. Then the moment was upon me. It was him straggling behind and stopping in front of the fortune teller's tent just as he did in my dream. As he took two steps toward the tent, I suddenly realized exactly why I was there.

I stepped toward my brother and a voice came from behind, "Where are you going Shirley Mae?"

I had no time nor any notion to reply as the sound of my name tore Larry's gaze from the seer to me even as she called out.
"Do you have any questions about your future, little man?"

He did not recognize me completely but enough to keep him from answering her and I knew that this was the reason I had to be here. I had to keep his faith in us from being destroyed by the faker.

I called to him, "Hey, big brother! I'm sorry you couldn't come with me." As I said the words, all else faded away and the only sound was my voice. He didn't speak but his eyes widened, and I could see that he recognized me. I took one more step to him and embraced him. I told him that it was truly me, that his stories about my life were true and he must keep telling them. I took a step back and asked him to look at me and to remember me, so I wouldn't be forgotten and finally that I loved him. As I stood there for a few moments in silence I could see a man coming from behind Larry and grabbing his shoulder.

At the exact same moment, a hand was on my shoulder as well, turning me away from Larry even as I heard him cry out, "I love you, Shirley Mae."

The hand belonged to Peggy Sue who looked truly concerned for me and my mental state. My eyes were only turned for a moment but when they turned back all was as it was before but there was no sign of Larry or his family.

8

For the next five years after the encounter with my little sister I wrote down all the stories instead of just telling them. I started from the beginning when she was in the water being rescued and worked diligently to catch up to the present day. By the time I was all caught up I was approaching my 15th birthday.

More than once I considered the timeline. I wondered and began to hope that since Shirley Mae was born on my 5th birthday and met me 5yrs to the day later on my tenth, could it be possible that she would appear again on my 15th birthday? The thought of this possibility helped me to maintain confidence in our connection. As could be expected most of my siblings grew doubtful and even weary of it all as they entered adulthood. It was easy for me to maintain an absolute mindset shortly after my experience at the carnival but with the passing of time and the memory of it fading evermore slightly each year it became more difficult. As I entered my teens and began to have more social experiences outside of my family, by which I mean girls, I found myself hesitant to talk about Shirley Mae, afraid of being labeled weird or worse. On the day of the carnival, I believed with absolute certainty that the experience was real, but now more than four years later, it would be so easy for me to tell myself that it was all an illusion like my father first suggested. It didn't help that, as the next years passed and Shirley Mae entered her teens, the stories became mundane. I suppose it was good that she was living in uninteresting times, but it grew more difficult to maintain my own interest let alone anyone else's. The solution was to change the story telling into a mere diary. It was easier that way.

On the day of my 15th birthday my family, as usual, had a party planned at our house with some of my friends invited to come. Unlike other years, however, I had requested that some of these friends be female with one in particular. Her name was Jill Jenkins but most of her friends called her J.J. She was my first real love, and I was totally enraptured by her. She stood an inch taller than me, but she didn't seem to mind. She was a slim blonde with the deepest of blue eyes and just enough tomboy in her to make her fun and in an inexplicable way, sexy. She drove me crazy. My parents and my siblings had agreed to make themselves scarce and as Tommy James and the Shondells belted out, "Hanky Panky" on the record player everything seemed to be going great. I had only been dating JJ for a short time and planned on asking her to be my steady girlfriend which means we would not date any other people. This, I was told, usually resulted in a more intimate relationship and as a healthy fifteen-year-old male I was extremely anxious to find out if that was true. The time seemed right, and I gave a nod toward my good friend Jimmy Daniels who was manning the player. He switched records and JJ and I began swaying as Percy Sledge sang, "When a Man Loves a Woman" which was the perfect fit. The plan was to lean back a little and when she looked at me, I would kiss her and then ask her. The scene had played over in my mind a thousand times in the past week, and I considered the plan flawless.

Instead, however, Robbie Burns' declaration "The best laid plans of mice and men" received another example of its accuracy at that moment. I leaned back and JJ looked at me and smiled but as I leaned in, and her eyes closed a hand tapped me on my shoulder.

It was an ambush with Danny Macon making the perfectly acceptable request to "cut in". It would have been considered an insult for me to refuse to step aside even under normal circumstances but with my being the host of the party refusing was absolutely not an option. It would have destroyed the moment anyway. JJ had the option to refuse but I knew she wouldn't. She didn't know what I had planned and would just see it as good manners to accept.

I moved to the side of the room next to Jimmy as I counted out thirty seconds which I calculated to be the minimum time deemed acceptable before cutting back in. I had reached twenty-eight seconds when another boy, Dave Hudson stepped up and tapped Danny on the shoulder and after a quick glance at each other switched out. I began the count again, only reaching twenty when another, Billy Barker, stepped up and I could see that the switch appeared almost rehearsed or at least planned with no words exchanged between Billy and Dave. That was enough for me, and I moved without counting and tapped Billy on the shoulder just as Mr. Sledge finished up. With the music stopped while the record was being changed and Billy's voice being higher than necessary, everyone turned as he spoke.

"I was just asking JJ if you had mentioned if you had seen your little sister today yet," he said. I had not spoken of Shirley Mae to JJ. In fact, I had not spoken of her for the entire 2 weeks that we were dating. As I said before, it was just easier.

"Hey that's right, today's your 15th birthday." Danny added with mock surprise.

"What are they talking about, Larry?" JJ asked.

"It's nothing, just something that happened to me five years ago." I offered, praying that the music would start up and I glanced toward Jimmy who heard what was going on and had stopped to listen. I shot a menacing look at him which he saw and immediately started to fumble with another record which he dropped.

"Oh, come on, Larry," Danny broke in. "Tell her how you saw your little sister five years ago who was, somehow, the same age as you at a carnival."
"Shut up, Macon," I threatened as I clenched my fists.

"What's the matter, Pickett? Is there some reason you don't want her to hear about your dead sister?"

I swung wildly at him at the words *dead sister*. The blow didn't land and in a moment, we were on the floor. He had the weight advantage and I quickly found myself being sat upon, pinned to the floor. It was humiliating. Jimmy stepped up with a feeble gesture of assistance, but Billy and Dave moved to stop him which was all it took. They also were bigger.

"Tell her, Pickett and I'll let you up." I was desperate to salvage some shred of dignity in the hopes that this would be over. "It was a long time ago and I can't really remember it all or even if it happened at all." I offered.

"Not good enough. JJ has a right to hear the whole story so let's have it." he countered.

"I'm telling you there's nothing to tell. I just had a little episode, probably the heat or something."

"Are you saying that you only imagined that you talked to your little sister, and it was all in your head?" he taunted.

"Yes, that's what I'm saying. She is dead and I know it. Now let me up."

He let me stand and I realized that there were tears rolling down my face. After a few moments everyone started filing out since it was obvious the party was over.

Even JJ left after offering a weak, "I'll call you later."

The apostle Peter could not have felt more shame after he denied his Lord three times than I felt as I sat there alone. Three times I could have told them all that it was all true and three times I denied it. The next day JJ called to ask how I was doing but I knew we weren't going to happen. I could hear it in her tone and phrasing. A few days later I saw her out with Danny and my shame instantly turned to anger. I swore to myself that I would not mention Shirley Mae again. I continued writing the stories, but they took a dark turn.

9

After my visit with Larry at the carnival My dreams stopped and that upset me greatly. I eventually reasoned that they had served their purpose which was to lead me to that place on that day to stop Larry's belief in my alternate life being shattered. My life became normal again. I would even say mediocre.

It was on the eve of my 15th birthday that the dreams started again. The first was truly upsetting and I called Peggy who still kept in touch albeit sporadically. Even though it was just a phone call I could picture the huge eye roll just by the faint groan and the patronization that followed.

"You know it could just be a regular dream like billions of people have every night, Shirl," she finally said impatiently.

"No, it was just like before except it wasn't enjoyable. In fact, it was terribly upsetting."

"OK, but why would they start up again after all this time?"

"I don't know, Peg. But I'm sure there must be a reason just like last time."

"Let's hear it then, Shirl. Tell me what was so upsetting about this dream."

"OK, but please don't interrupt until I finish." She agreed and I began.

"I found myself in a house where a party was going on. At first, I didn't recognize anyone. Young people our age were dancing and seemed to be friends just having a good time but I still had an inexplicable feeling of dread. As in the dream I had the night before my 10th birthday I was able to move around in the room and no one could see me. After a minute or two I spotted Larry dancing with a pretty blonde girl just as the song came to an end and a slow one began. They embraced and I started to think my uneasiness would prove unwarranted. Suddenly some big guy tapped Larry on the shoulder to cut in and I could see that he wasn't happy about stepping aside. He moved to the side of the room where I joined him without his knowing and soon another guy cut in replacing the first. I could sense the frustration and anger rising in my brother as he quietly counted for some reason. He reached twenty when yet another guy stepped up to switch out with the second, which proved too much for Larry to tolerate. The sense of disaster returned, and I tried to speak to him like before to warn him. It was like an invisible wall was between us and I remembered that this was just a dream. I wasn't actually at the party like I was at the carnival. The one who had been dancing with the girl asked Larry about his little sister and at first, I thought there had been an addition to his family. That proved not to be the case when the big one broke in. First, he confirmed what I suspected that it was Larry's fifteenth birthday and then mentioned the carnival encounter. I realized at that point what was going on. Larry was being mocked for his belief in me and was about to lose control. The words, dead sister, seemed to be the tipping point and, suddenly, they were on the floor with the big guy on top. He was demanding that Larry tell the story. Larry hedged, obviously embarrassed by the situation and by the story we shared. The bully asked if he had only imagined that he'd talked to his little sister and that it was all in his head. When I heard the reply, I knew why the dreams had stopped until now. He confirmed that's what he was saying, and he knew I was dead. Then he yelled at him to let him up. Maybe it was spoken in total frustration, but even so, the tone told me that he believed it or at least he wanted to believe it and what's more he, in some way, regretted our connection altogether. I could see the anger in his face that had been redirected from his assailant to me or at least the memory of me. The realization that the connection we had, whatever it was, had been possibly severed was enough to jolt me awake. It was the first time in my life that I woke up with tears on my face."

Peggy Sue finally broke in asking," Are you alright Shirley Mae?" Even over the phone she could tell how upset I was, and her tone changed. She tried to be comforting and that made me even more emotional.

I finally pulled myself together and after she wished me a happy birthday we hung up. I thought of the possibility of being surprised by my parents. Maybe someone had invited me to a party and it would set the stage for another encounter like the day of the carnival. As I made an attempt to eat the tall stack of blueberry pancakes before me it became apparent that there was no surprise to come. In fact, I could sense that my parents were holding something back from me. They both wore smiles, but I could tell they were just going through the motions for my sake. They didn't want to ruin my big day and so they saved the surprise for the next day.

In the morning my parents were waiting for me at the breakfast table. They wore serious faces, and I remembered the uneasy feeling the morning before of them holding back something. After an attempt at small talk, they let me have it.

We had to move back to New York, which wasn't all bad. At least I would be reunited with Peggy Sue. That was not the bad part. My father was a Korean war veteran. He was drafted a year before my birth. His college education qualified him for officer status, and he served two years. While on leave he met my mother who was a nurse at a MASH unit. Shortly after that she was pregnant, and they were married. The order of the two events are, to this day, sketchy. She came back stateside where he joined her after doing his two years. Over the two years he quickly shot up in rank from a second Lieutenant to Major and earned a distinguished service medal among others. Now something was going on over in Asia in a place called Vietnam and my father was called up for a special assignment, or something like that. There wasn't to be a general draft for another three years, but when they called, he agreed to go. That's what his generation did, apparently. He left two weeks later. The return to New York was necessary so we would be close to my mom's parents and her sister, Aunt Shirley.

We received a few letters and one phone call over the next four months. Strict security reasons were blamed for the sparse correspondence. Then, finally we got word that dad was scheduled for leave during the Christmas school break. My mom and I fanatically decorated the house in anticipation of his arrival. We wanted everything to be perfect when he got there. We usually trimmed the tree on Christmas eve, and we were trying to wait for him but it was five hours past his estimated time of arrival and we had to start without him. We were almost finished except for the beautiful glass star which had been in the family for three generations. It was always left to the end and was only brought out then because of its fragility and sentimental value. My mother went downstairs to where we stored the decorations to get it while I went to get the step stool from the front hall closet when the doorbell rang. I remember thinking that dad must have left his keys in Nam when I flung the door open ready to jump on him and smother him with hugs and kisses. Instead, there were two men in uniform standing erect as if at attention, but neither was my father. I assumed they were friends of his who were to meet him here and they had not been warned of his tardiness.

As I stood in the doorway processing the situation the question came that made my heart stop.

"Is your mother at home?"

The word mother was supposed to be father in my mind. It was supposed to be," Is your father at home?' but it wasn't.

My mind was locked in the moment, and I couldn't speak. A moment later I was snapped out of it by the sound of breaking glass coming from behind me and the cry that would be in my memory evermore.

Dad's chopper had just taken off to bring him to the Saigon airport and then home when it crashed due to mechanical failure. The irony of having survived Korea and six months in Nam then to fall victim to a bad engine part only made the tragedy even more horrendous. The funeral was on New Year's Eve which in hindsight was very fitting since my life changed drastically. It felt like a book had finished and a new one had begun.

10

For five years I was true to my oath and did not mention Shirley Mae to anyone, not even my family. With each year her memory grew fainter. The memory of my humiliating 15th birthday had a profound effect on my mindset and therefore my character or at least the character I wished to portray. I had learned that good guys definitely *do* finish last and if I wanted to be a winner in life, I would have to be tougher. My new persona seemed to pay great dividends in respect from others as well as in the romance department. J.J even started to notice the change in me. Just over a year after dumping me she approached me and let her feelings be known.

The old Larry would have jumped at the chance to be with her, but I had built up my confidence to a point of arrogance that only a sixteen-year-old could achieve. I snubbed her with great satisfaction.

The 60's ushered in a new era that was made for the young. *Make love not war* and *turn on and drop out* became mantras of the youth movement. By 1967 the youth had embraced the drug culture as a means of rebellion. If you wanted to be anyone you needed to embrace it as well. If you mastered the hippy vernacular, wore the right clothes, and did the right drugs the teenage social world would be yours. By the time I was eighteen I was getting high most days and began to drink on top of that. The person I had become bore no semblance to the boy who told his little sister that he loved her eight years earlier and who had sworn to her that he would keep her memories alive by telling stories about her life. I was slipping slowly into a dark place and directed my jadedness toward everyone around me including the memory of Shirley Mae.

I did, however, continue to write stories in my journal but I didn't know if I was just making them up or if they were actually true stories of Shirley Mae's life. I wasn't even sure why I continued to write about her. I think it was more habit than anything else, but it did seem therapeutic at times and the need to continue became a compulsion, a compulsion I resented.

Somehow despite my new habits I managed to finish high school and get accepted to a college with a high acceptance rate. The main requirement was your application and your ability to sign your name correctly on the tuition check, but it got me out of the house and the chance to experience college life. It also offered some protection from the possible Vietnam draft rumored to be coming soon. The courses were a joke and that left unlimited time to party which, combined with my already heavy drug use and drinking, created a perfect storm for disaster.

***

For three years after my 15th birthday, I rarely dreamt of my brother and when I did the dreams were fragmented, filled only with vague images that haunted my sleep. The only constant was Larry who was always standing in the midst of some peril. It was consistently dark, but the situation would change. He would be at the edge of some precipice one night and drowning in the next. There was never any detail to the scene, only a sense of terror and when I awoke, one of foreboding.

They remained this way until one night in the wee hours of my 18th birthday. That night, as I dreamt, I found myself driving almost blind down a steep hill at night in a torrential downpour that was overwhelming the car's wipers. As I tried to stop, the dash clock seemed to glare at me showing 2:15 as if telling me it was important. The car slowed, seemingly without any effort from me and I spotted a vehicle at the bottom. It was smoking and the front of it was nearly obliterated. It had crashed through the guard rail that bordered the turn in the flattening road. I came to a stop a few feet behind the wreck and got out almost involuntarily. What I mean is I knew I had to go and look inside but I was terrified to do so. The sky seemed to open up even more and I was soaked in seconds. I tried to wipe the rain from my face and discovered I was wearing glasses. I removed them and looked at them for a moment, bewildered, never having the need before. I moved to the driver's door to see if there was anyone there. Between the rain and the night, it was impossible to see clearly as I tried the door. It had been badly damaged and would not budge.

As I wiped the water from the window in a desperate hope of getting a glimpse inside something or someone moved.

I called out, "Hello, can you hear me?"

The reply was barely audible and what was discernible was incoherent like the ramblings of a drunk. I looked back up the hill hoping someone would be coming but there was no one.

"I'm going to go and," *get help*, was what I was going to say when flames exploded from under what was left of the front end. I felt the heat from the flames as I began pounding on the window shouting,

"You need to get out now. Can you hear me? Get out!"

The scream that came from inside the car forced me to step back as the panic rose inside me. I'm not certain but I think I knew who it was before he turned toward the window. Even with his face being contorted in pain there was no doubt it was Larry. He was now totally conscious and his voice clearly recognizable.

"Help me, please!" he screamed, without really seeing me.

"I'm here, Larry and I'll get you out, " I cried back to him.

Larry suddenly stopped. His face became peaceful as he recognized me.

Tiger eyes were the last words I heard before waking in my bed, soaking wet.

My mother, awakened by my cries, was seated at my bedside with her hand on my face. She said I was burning up and that I had sweat completely through my night clothes. Of course, a fever would explain the intense dream and the wet clothes, but I knew it was something more. A warning perhaps of a dark future in which Larry and I are somehow connected.

***

Six months later, while I was on Christmas break from my freshman year of college, my mother had a stroke and had to be hospitalized for six weeks. The doctors said she may make a full recovery, or she may not. Only time would tell. When she came home, she needed a lot of help and money became very tight. I had to drop out of college and start working full time to pay the bills. I hadn't bothered getting a driver's license up to this point. Like many New Yorkers, I preferred public transit over constant traffic jams, but at that point it had become a necessity.

During the eye test for my license, I was informed that my eyes were not quite up to the minimum standard and I would require corrective lenses to drive.

11

The memory of Shirley Mae was all but gone during my first year of college and was completely wiped out by December first of my second year by a tsunami of recreational pharmaceuticals and booze.

As I sat in the dean's office on that day awaiting him to show up and conduct, what was sure to be, a firm showing of the door to me, I could hear a commotion in the hallway. I stepped out and grabbed a freshman hurrying past and asked what was going on.

"Nixon has done it." he yelled.

"Who did what? I responded not knowing what he was talking about.

Exasperated at my ignorance he shouted at me as he pulled away from my grip.

"President Nixon's draft lottery took place today and we may be going to Nam."

The freshman's anxiety turned out not to be totally justified. Although the lottery made it possible for anyone to be picked for duty, college students could still apply for a student deferment which meant that they could wait and serve their tour at peace time. That was the good news. The bad news, for me at least, was that my suspicions were correct and the dean, when he finally showed up, wasted no time telling me my presence was no longer welcome at their place of higher learning. Apparently, even though it was very easy to get into this place and the scholastic standards were a joke, they drew a line with students coming to their classes high especially when a stash was found in that students locker. Who knew searching a student's locker was totally legal?

I was home in a couple of days. My family was understandably upset, and I was told to, "Get a job."

That wasn't a problem with so many young men already serving their country over eight thousand miles away. I found one in a week. After starting the job, its requirements and because I was back living at home, my drug use and drinking dropped off significantly and my head became a little clearer. Don't get me wrong, I still did my share but it was mostly on weekends and at a much more controllable rate. It was during this time that I started to write complete stories again in my Shirley Mae Journal. I looked back at my writings from the previous few years, and they were almost incomprehensible. They were merely random expressions of the dark persona that I had chosen for myself. It was obvious that I had poured every negative feeling I felt into the scribblings even though it was all my own fault that my life had spiraled downward. If my stories were an account of my sister's second life, then it was definitely a trouble filled one.

My draft card showed up shortly after I started my job and seven months later a letter telling me to report for duty July 28th, two days after my twentieth birthday. That only gave me about a week, so the job immediately became history, and my focus was on my twentieth birthday/going away bash. I figured it may be my last hurrah.

***

Aunt Shirley had become an almost permanent fixture at our place once my mother came home. We could have been merely ships in the night, trading off like shift workers to stay with my mom but we genuinely liked each other, and we quickly became very close. It may have been that we both realized we shared a common feature in our lives, tragedy. She was widowed by thirty-five and lost her only daughter ten years later. We spent a lot of time together and had many long talks. As this bond grew stronger during those first few months after mom's stroke, I felt the urge to speak to her about my dreams. Peggy Sue was away at college with little time for me and I never felt right talking to my mother about what I believed especially after dad died.

Now, of course, that was totally out of the question. Aunt Shirley was easy to talk to. One afternoon she arrived a little earlier than usual and caught me crying.

"What's all this, then, my miss Mae?" she asked.

In spite of being my aunt's namesake or perhaps because of it my Aunt Shirley always called me Mae. She was the only one who did, and I guess it was another reason our relationship seemed special.

"It's nothing", I replied feeling a little embarrassed at being caught in tears.

"Oh, come now, Mae, one thing I've learned over the years is that when someone is crying it's never about nothing so let's have it and maybe I can help."

I told her everything right from the time I woke up in the water fifteen years earlier to the carnival visit with Larry and what I believed. Some of it she had heard from my mom, but she sat patiently while I poured out the entire story including the dream about Larry's fifteenth birthday party. Finally, I told her about my dream on the eve of my eighteenth birthday.

"I think it is some type of warning or omen," I explained.

"Do you really believe you are his little sister of a former life, Mae?"

"I don't know if it is a former life, a parallel life or something else altogether, Aunt Shirley, but one thing I do know for sure is my life is somehow connected to Larry's, whoever he is."

"Do you remember, Mae, that I taught high school physics before I was married?"

"My mom told me you did but by the time I knew you, you had stopped teaching."

"Yes of course, that's right. I've always had an interest in the sciences, and I remember reading an article in a science journal while waiting at my dentist's office about ten years ago. It was about a theory a man named Hugh Everett III put forward about parallel universes. I didn't really understand it entirely, but I figure if a renowned scientist and official smart guy like him thinks there could be more than one world, then who are we to say there isn't. Besides there are all kinds of things we don't understand and if you say you have lived two lives then I say anything is possible."

"Thank you, Aunty for listening and not thinking I'm crazy. I'd write it all off myself as a loss of sanity if it wasn't for the encounter at the carnival. Not only did my dream the night before predict it, but it was so real. I mean I actually hugged him and spoke to him, and he spoke back. I know it wasn't my imagination."

"I believe you, Mae and what's more I think I can see something else that you may be too close to have noticed."

My aunt paused here before going on as if rethinking the wisdom of telling me. She had a concerned look on her face and did not speak until I prompted.

"What is it?" I asked, starting to feel concerned myself.

"It's just that," she finally started, "have you never noticed how your life was going so well until your fifteenth birthday?"

I had to think for a moment and then responded, "Yes, I suppose. That was when my parents told me about my dad having to go away. Actually you're right, nothing has been the same since. So, what are you thinking?

"Well, have you not noticed it was right after your dream of Larry on his fifteenth birthday. The timing cannot be a coincidence."

"What are you saying, Aunt Shirley? Do you think all the tragedy is somehow connected to Larry? That sounds even crazier than what I told you. I mean, it's one thing to believe there is some kind of connection between the two of us and another to believe one world caused things to happen in another."

"No, Mae. I'm not saying that, but if you look at that dream and the last one where you find your brother in a twisted wreck it's obvious that his life has gone downhill as well in the past five years."

There was a pause while I absorbed what my aunt had told me and while she gave me time to do so. Finally, she broke the silence.

"Listen, Mae, you keep saying there is some kind of connection between the two of you. Maybe because of this connection Larry's life somehow affects yours."

"How could that be?" was all I could respond with. I was too busy thinking back to all the dreams and their timeline. I started looking at them in the light of this new proposal.

I remembered that Larry appeared to be a happy person when he was younger, and this seemed to be confirmed at our encounter at the carnival. Even in the years after that, as far as I could tell from my dreams, he seemed happy right up until his fifteenth birthday. Then it all changed. It was then that his attitude toward me or at least the belief in me changed.

"Mae, are you alright?" Aunt Shirley finally said.

She pulled me back from my thoughts.

"I think you may be right, Aunty. Larry is affecting my life in some direct way."

"What way is that, Mae?"

"I'm not sure, but I keep going back to the dream that seemed to predict the future event. Remember? I told you. The one in which Larry told the story about me and my parents moving to Toronto."

"Yes I remember but I thought you weren't sure it was a prediction or just a wild coincidence."

"Yes that's right, but after what you pointed out to me about my life going downhill at the same time as Larry's I'm sure there is a definite cause and effect."

"How can you be so sure, Mae?" my aunt interjected in an

attempt to slow me down. Her voice seemed concerned, but I ignored it.

"I don't know how but somehow it is perfectly clear to me."

"What is, Mae? You're starting to scare me a little. Look at me, Mae!

I turned to look at her and realized I had been staring into space. The revelation had come to me with such clarity it seemed to be supernatural intervention. I was in awe.

I stared into the scared face of my Aunty and asked, "Don't you see? There can be no other explanation."

"What is it, Mae? Tell me, please."

I paused for a few moments, afraid to put what I was thinking into words.

"What is it, Mae? " she repeated in a softer, more comforting voice. She could see the conflict going on in me.

Finally, I said what I could hardly believe but knew to be true, "It's Larry's stories, Aunty. I don't think he's writing stories about my life. I think he's creating my life with his stories."

12

Monday, July 26th, 1971, started out uneventful. At least it did for me. I decided to start my 20th birthday celebration by sleeping in. I figured I was going to need my energy for the partying that I intended to be doing into the wee hours. I sat eating breakfast around 9:30 while my parents were glued to the TV set watching NASA launch yet another Apollo rocket to the moon.

It seems that my 20th birthday was no match in excitement. At least not until the bucket of bolts got off the ground. I had almost finished my 3rd and last bowl of Wheaties when my father came into the kitchen for another cup of coffee.

As he poured it and with his back to me, he asked, "You got plans for tonight? He turned and saw I had stuffed my mouth full of cereal and decided to continue. "It's just that Gord and Mark said they may stop by and wish you a happy 20th if you were going to be around."

"What time?" was all I could manage to squeak out while still chewing.

"They said around six. Your mom and I got a cake and we thought we could, you know do the whole Happy Birthday thing. That is if you don't think you're too old for that kind of stuff."

"No, I'm not too old and thanks for the cake but I'll be meeting some friends at five for a bite and they have some kind of festivities planned for me. Could we do the cake thing tomorrow? I don't have to report till Wednesday."

"Well, it's your birthday so I guess you can do what you want.

I'll see if your brothers can come tomorrow instead."

"Thanks. Any chance I can borrow the car?"

There was a full 3 second pause while he sighed but he finally caved. "I suppose but if you decide to tie one on, just take a cab home and we'll get the car in the morning. Deal?"

"Thanks," I agreed.

We hadn't been very close since I got kicked out of college but with my being drafted and it being my twentieth he was almost warm. It reminded me of how we used to be when I was young. Most young people have some issues with their parents but ours were significant. Being the youngest just widened the gap between his and my generation. Basically, we didn't understand each other and our perspectives on Nam made it worse.

***

I spent the afternoon packing for Wednesday. My mom came up to lend a hand and to spend some time with me. She wasn't the same since my brother David shipped out. My other brothers, Gord and Mark were still Stateside, but David volunteered. He probably wanted to make my dad proud, and I think my mom blamed my dad a little for David's decision. She was very emotional since then and she had trouble looking me in the face without welling up. It was not a good time.

I had about another hour to kill before heading out and I filled it by writing one more chapter in the life of Shirley Mae. I had finished the last chapter with a cliffhanger about her finding her mother unconscious on the bathroom floor. As I began to write, I was conflicted as to how to deal with the situation. Should I have her mother succumb to her illness or have her recover? Somehow the question of life or death seemed more real now that I would be facing it myself in a short time. The power that I would normally feel when making a decision such as this was not there. I could not decide and so I left her hanging on to life after major surgery.

I left the house around 4:30 to meet my friends, Bill and Jack, but it wasn't at a restaurant as I had alluded to earlier to my father. We went straight to the bar and our time there began as it would end. With shots and beers and nobody counting.

***

I did not dream of my brother at all after the night of my great revelation. I thought it may have been some type of defense mechanism as if my mind, after realizing the truth about the dreams had shut them out. My Aunt and I continued to trade off around the clock to care for my mother. As time passed it became easier to dismiss the notion of my life being merely a story in somebody's book in another world. I happily began to believe that it was a foolish idea. Then on the eve of my 20th birthday my mother collapsed while in the washroom. I found her on the floor unconscious. The ambulance was there in minutes and within an hour she was in an operating room. It was another stroke. It was more severe and had caused bleeding in the brain. Four hours later she laid in ICU and the surgeon told me it could go either way. The staff said I could not sit in the ICU and told me my mother would not gain consciousness for many hours. They suggested I go home and get some sleep and return in the morning rested. My Aunt Shirley, who had joined me at the hospital also said I should go, and she would stay. I reluctantly took their advice.

When I got home it was late and I laid down on my bed without changing. The night was filled with disjointed visions of glasses clinking and loud voices. They seemed to be singing one moment then shouting in anger the next. I realized I was at a bar but not one I had ever been to before. It was crowded with drunken men full of bluster and booze. They all suddenly turned and stared at me as if surprised I was there, as if I should be somewhere else.

They moved toward me shouting, "Get out! Get out! You're not supposed to be here. Look at the time. You will be late."

They were pointing at a clock behind the bar. It was identical to the clock in my mother's car, and it showed two o'clock. I turned, running through the door but only to find myself in my mother's car once again driving blind in pouring rain down the same hill as in the dream exactly two years before. It was playing out the same and as I strained my eyes peering through the night the wreck came into view. I had just decided in my mind to do whatever it took to save my brother, this time, when I was jarred awake by the hand of my aunt.

It was morning and she had come to tell me about the situation at the hospital. "Wake up Mae!" she shouted at me as she gently shook me. The abrupt awakening disoriented me for a few seconds.

"Aunt Shirley? Where are we?" I stammered, still not fully awake.

"You're at home, Mae. You were thrashing and mumbling in your sleep something about your brother. Are you alright?"

"Yes, I think so, now. Thanks for waking me. How is my mom doing?"

"She is stable and out of the I.C.U. but they are moving her to the General where they specialize in brain injuries. They're doing that as we speak. That's why I'm here with you now. It seemed like you were having a nightmare, probably about your mom, I suppose."

"No, Aunty, it wasn't exactly a nightmare. It wasn't pleasant either, but it seemed to be another warning."

"What do you mean, another warning?" My aunt asked as a concerned look formed on her face.

"It started in a bar and people were shouting at me that I would be late. It wasn't that frightening, but I could feel a sense of urgency growing within me. I still didn't know where I was supposed to be, but I ran out through a door and immediately found myself driving in my mother's car. From there it was the same as the dream I had told you about. You remember, the one where Larry is trapped in a wrecked car. You woke me just as I was approaching the wreck."

The concerned look remained on my aunt's face, but she turned to her left, obviously trying to recall the details of the dream. She finally responded, "Maybe it would have been better if I hadn't woken you.

"No, I'm glad you did. It would have probably played out the same as the first time and I wasn't prepared to help him. I'll be ready next time."

This startled my aunt, and her voice showed it, "Wait a minute, Mae. Did you just hear yourself? I don't think you're quite awake yet. You realize that you are talking about something that has only happened in your head, don't you?"

"Of course, I do, " I quickly responded, "but it's the timing that tells me it's more."

"What do you mean, Mae? I don't understand."

"I had this dream exactly two years ago, or at least the part when I came upon Larry in the wrecked car."

"Maybe that's the answer, Mae," my aunt quickly jumped in. "Maybe you had the date on your mind or at least in your subconscious."

"No, Aunty, I had no inkling of what the date was until a few moments ago and my mind has been totally fixated on my mother, as well. I had even forgotten that today is my 20th birthday."

"Ok, Mae, but even if there was some supernatural connection and I'm not saying there is, how can you save him? You don't know where or when this accident is supposed to happen."

"I know that it's at night during a torrential downpour and minutes before 2:15 am."

"Well, I see there is no dissuading you so we should just put it aside for now. You should get showered and dressed and get over to the General as soon as you can. I'm going home to bed but call me if there is any change in your mom's condition no matter what the time is."

"I will Aunt Shirley."

She left and I showered, dressed, threw a bowl of cereal into my face, and took a coffee with me.

***

I was halfway to the General when the traffic slowed. A flagman was motioning all the eastbound traffic to turn left. The road was temporarily closed for construction. As I slowly passed him, I asked if I would come back to this road and told him where I was going. He assured me I would if I followed the signs. The detour road was unfamiliar to me. It was winding and hilly. As I was about to come out of an s-curve I was suddenly facing a long steep hill. I glanced to my left at a somewhat familiar guardrail. I was flooded with an overwhelming feeling of Déjà Vu. A horn blasted from behind me, and I realized I had strayed onto the wrong side of the road while staring at the rail. I pulled over to the shoulder and got out. I stared at the guardrail. I told myself that it looked like a million other guardrails in America, but the Déjà Vu persisted.

There was no way to tell if it was the same hill with the same curve at the bottom bordered by the same guardrail as in my dream, especially considering that in my dream it was night and pouring rain. I got back in my car and drove up the familiar looking hill. It was almost noon before I got to my mother's room. She was sleeping peacefully. I had brought a book to read but I couldn't finish a page without my mind drifting back to my brother and the feeling of urgency returned.

13

Bill and Jack bought me my first couple of drinks and when they let everyone in the bar know I was shipping out the day after tomorrow, others offered as well. I was having one of the best times I'd ever had. While the men were buying drinks, women were asking me to dance. It seemed everyone in the bar was determined to see me off in grand fashion. The time passed quickly with the last call being announced much earlier than I would have liked. There was no way to tell how much liquor I had consumed but it was obvious I was in no shape to drive, and neither were the two friends who were still with me as closing time neared.

The bar had pretty much emptied out and we were about to call a cab when things went south in a hurry. A small group of four sturdy looking youths approached us. It was obvious that they were feeling no pain as well.

The largest of the four put his face ridiculously close to mine and said, "So you're a big man going off to kill babies, are you?"

It was obvious that they were spoiling for a fight, but I could see no reason on earth why.

I moved my head back and replied, "What? "

The big guy moved his face toward me again, almost touching my nose with his. He looked like he was about to repeat his question when Jack squeezed between us and while wearing a pleasant smile and employing his winning way he said, "Whoa, let's settle down, guys. We're not looking for trouble and we were about to leave anyway."

The close talker pushed Jack aside without taking his eyes off me and shouted, "Have you ever heard of Jeff Miller?" and then without waiting for my reply, "How about Kent State? Have you heard of that, baby killer?"

Bill spoke up this time replying for me. "Everybody knows about the Kent State shootings. What's it got to do with us?"

Big guy finally took his eyes off mine to answer Bill's question.

"Jeff was my best friend and they shot him for protesting Nam and you assholes just spent the night celebrating this guy going over there like it was some kind of honor of something."

I finally figured out what was going on through my drunken fog and resented his saying that I was celebrating going off to war. I found my tongue and opened my mouth to protest but the only thing to come out after *I don't* was about a half-gallon of projectile vomit. This did not help the situation at all.

"Run!" was the only thing I heard and to this day I'm not sure if it was Jack or Bill who yelled it. I am, however, pretty sure it wasn't any of the four sturdy youths. The next few minutes were kind of a blur. I do remember Jack grabbing my left arm and Bill grabbing my right and the three of us crashing through a set of rather heavy doors to an awaiting torrential downpour.

Unfortunately, while Jack and Bill used their free hand to do so I had no free hand and I think I used my forehead. There was a space of time after that in which I have no recollection at all. I was awakened by rain drops coming through my father's partially opened back seat window. I was lying on the seat with a small lump in the middle of my forehead which would seem to confirm my suspicion concerning the door opening.

I was debating whether to roll over and go back to sleep when I spotted the car keys on the floor. I guess they were thrown in through the window which would explain why it was left open a crack. I took my discovery of the keys as a sign from God that I was meant to drive home and reasoned, who am I to argue with divine wisdom?

It was still teeming rain, but it had let up somewhat and I was not that far from home. I also factored into my decision to drive home the distinct possibility that I was probably going to be shot at in Nam and compared that to the dangers of the road. After weighing everything in my booze-soaked mind, I grabbed the keys off the floor and climbed into the front without getting out and into the driver's seat.

After getting the key into the ignition, which was no mean feat, and brought the engine to life the dash lit up and reminded me to turn on the headlights. I looked down to position my hand on the stick and looked past it to see the now illuminated dash clock. It showed 1:30.

The parking lot was empty which was fortunate because I probably would have hit anything that was even remotely near me. As I made my way tentatively through the streets the rain worsened. I remember thinking that it was a good thing. That with the terrible visibility any cop that happened by would not question my turtling along.

I began to not feel well. My stomach had decided it wanted to purge what little remained in it. I pulled over quickly, opened my car door and simultaneously threw up. I got about eighty percent of it out of the car. The stench was overwhelming and despite the weather I leaned across and partially opened the passenger window. Looking out as I did, I spotted an unfamiliar storefront that told me that I was not on the right road. I must have missed a turn, I reasoned.

I made a u-turn and started back in the direction I came. After two or three more wrong turns I came upon a "road closed" sign and another bearing a large black arrow demanding I turn right. It was obvious I was totally lost and decided I would park and sleep it off as soon as I could find a suitable place. With each mile the rain seemed to worsen and the terrain more rural. I started down a long hill that was at least straight and I picked it up a little, anxious to end the nightmare. With only fields around me there was little for orientation, and I picked up speed unaware that I was slowly accelerating into dangerous speeds. I thought the rain was getting worse when in fact my increasing speed was the cause of my ever-decreasing visibility. I was straining through the windshield into the rain and darkness and then it was there. With little warning the hill flattened, and the road turned simultaneously. I buried the brake and the car immediately started to fishtail. With only a split second to react I turned the wheel hard right to try to keep control, but it was no use. My speed had climbed too high, and the road was too wet.

I smashed almost head on into the guardrail that bordered the road with the front driver's corner taking slightly more than its share of the brunt. As if in slow motion I can see the next second or two in my mind. My head hit the windshield in the same instant I felt the steering wheel pound me in my chest forcing me back against the seat and knocking all the air out of me. Then everything went black.

I can vaguely recall hearing a voice calling out to me as if trying to awaken me. It was indiscernible but I wanted to reach out to it as one would a lifeline. An explosion suddenly brought me back to near full consciousness. That is when the unimaginable pain flooded through me, and a shriek came out of me that sounded like someone else was screaming it. I cried out to God, "Help me please!"

***

I had not left my mother's side all that day but for a few minutes, when necessary, to eat and washroom visits. Hardly a great way to spend one's 20th birthday but I would not utter a single syllable of complaint if only my mother would open her eyes and speak a few words to me.

My Aunt Shirley called the hospital to get a message to me. She said if I was alright, she would do some things that needed doing and come to relieve me later that night. It mattered little to me because I wasn't planning on going anywhere, at least not until my mother was awake. I managed to get a vending machine sandwich in me around three o'clock and a ward nurse surprised me with a meal tray at six. It went down better than I expected and took another shot at reading my book.

***

The summer sun was slowly allowing the night to come. I remember a short period of total darkness so I'm guessing I fell asleep around ten.

I was suddenly walking on a beach and the sand and breeze were warm. I laid down on the sand, eyes closed and felt totally at peace, a feeling I had not felt for as long as I could remember. I laid there as an infant would, both helpless but somehow unafraid.

As I lay there, I could sense the sun being blocked and I opened my eyes to slits and squinted at a somewhat familiar silhouette. As my eyes adjusted, he moved closer, further blocking the sun until I could fully open them.

I stared for a few moments and then declared, "I know you."

It was more than just recognizing a face and not remembering where you had met before. He was not just a familiar face. I knew him and about him, somehow. I remember I had been resting just as I was now but a lifetime ago. He had spoken to me then to tell me what I needed to know. He had prepared me for something to come and comforted me. Now he was here again and the feelings I felt then washed over me just like before. I would've stayed there forever if I could.

"It is time," was all he said.

The next moment I heard a voice calling but seemingly from a great distance. I didn't want to leave this place and I called out protesting, "No!"

The voice was suddenly next to me jarring me awake.

"Shirley Mae, wake up! Are you OK?"

Once again, my aunt had pulled me from my sleep. My face was wet with tears but not from sorrow. They came from the deep emotional experience that confirmed the belief and connection that Larry and I shared.

"I'm alright Aunty. I'm more than alright."

As I quickly turned to look at the monitors to see if there was any change in my mother's condition, my aunt explained her concern,

"You were calling out in your sleep and crying at the same time. I don't think I've ever seen anything like it before in my life. Are you sure you're OK, Mae?

"Yes, don't worry," I replied with my mind still partially yearning for the place I had just been taken from. I could see that my mother was still holding her own and I was able to finally give my full attention as my aunt continued.

"I got here a few hours ago but you were sleeping so soundly I didn't want to wake you. I thought you may have finally slept through the night but now that you are awake, I think you should go and get a good rest in your own bed. I'll stay with your mom, of course."

"No, Aunt Shirley," I replied firmly, "I won't leave until my mother is awake and I know she is out of the woods."

"Listen to me, Mae. We have no idea when that is going to happen. It could be days or longer. She is going to need you more than ever when she does wake up. Exhausting yourself like this is not helping her. It is time for you to go."

I was waiting for her to finish her argument and was going to protest until her last declaration or at least the first three words, *it is time.*

I had opened my mouth to speak but stopped when the words and their significance struck me. I glanced at the clock on the wall. It showed 1:40. I stood up suddenly, moved quickly to the window and pulled aside the blind as my startled aunt looked on. It was the darkest night I had ever seen, made even more so by the torrential rain and wind pounding against the glass.

"What is it, Mae?"

"I have to go." I replied as I picked up my coat and started for the door.

"Wait, Mae," my aunt said as she stood and grabbed my arm stopping me. "I had no idea the weather had turned so frightful. Maybe you should wait until it lets up."

"No, I have to go now, or it will be too late."

"Where, Mae? For the love of God, where could you possibly need to be that would take you out into a night like this?"

I stopped for a moment when I saw the legitimate concern on her face. I smiled, kissed her cheek, and hugged her. As I did I whispered softly into her ear, "I think you know, Aunty and I have no choice."
"But that was just a dream," she said weakly, sensing that there was no stopping me.

I leaned back and saw tears running down her face. I kissed her cheek once more and as I turned toward the door I said, "No, Aunt Shirley it was more, much much more."

When I reached the main lobby I stopped at a payphone, dropped a dime, and dialed. When I could hear it starting to ring, the phone at the front desk directly across from me began to ring as well.

"Hello, General Hospital, can I help you?"

I turned my head and spoke into my jacket trying to speak as loud as I could without the nurse who answered the phone hearing me.

"I need an ambulance right away on the detour road west of the hospital."

"Please try to calm down and tell me what has happened."

I raised my voice slightly trying to convey the urgency of the emergency that hadn't happened yet. "There's a car crash and a man is trapped inside."

"Where exactly did this crash happen, ma'am?"

"I don't know the name of the road but it's the one being used to detour off the main road west of the hospital. Please hurry, I'm calling from someone's house that I only found after looking for a while and the man was in rough shape when I left him."

"Okay, we'll dispatch an ambulance right away but with the storm we can't give you an ETA. What is your name, ma'am?"

14

I hung up the phone without answering and ran through the hospital's front doors just as a sheet of lightning lit up the sky showing the ferocity of the storm. I stopped short of the downpour trying to recall the exact location of my mother's car. I pulled my jacket over my head and made a dash to where I guessed it was. I was lucky and found it without a problem and miraculously avoided dropping my keys out of my shaking hands. As I smoothly glided them into the ignition I glanced down at the clock. It showed 1:55.

As I pulled out, I put the wipers on full which gave me acceptable visibility but of course I was only crawling as I maneuvered out of the lot. There was no one at the lot attendant's shack probably because of the hour which saved another precious minute or two. Even with the wipers killing themselves to keep up I had to keep my speed below 30mph, or I would be virtually driving blind. There was no way I could be sure how long Larry had been trapped in the car in my dream before I came upon him, but it couldn't have been more than a few minutes. A quick estimate in my head deduced a crash time of 2:10.

I had finally arrived at the detour road at 2:04 when the idea came to me. *Is it possible to get there before the accident? Would it be possible to somehow prevent it?* The rain had slowed slightly and so I leaned forward to get every possible inch of visibility and pushed the envelope to the limit. I had only traveled this road once before in the opposite direction and with the darkness and rain nothing could be seen that would tell me where on this nightmare road I was. Despite this when I came to the long straight hill of my dreams, I recognized it instantly. I sped up trusting the road would be straight and seconds later my heart skipped a beat. Taillights appeared through the void not more than a hundred yards ahead of me. It had to be him. I hadn't seen another car on this road since I pulled onto it. I sped up again throwing caution to the wind and leaned on the horn without letting up. I had a split second of hope when the brake lights in front of me came on. I thought, *yes, he heard me, he's stopping* but it was not the case. It fishtailed to the right allowing its headlights to illuminate the red stickered guard rail warning of the curve at the bottom of the hill then back slightly. I let my hand off the horn just in time to hear the bone chilling impact. It was so loud I could hear it over the rain and through my closed windows.

This time, unlike in my dream there was no confusion in my mind. I knew exactly what was going on. I was meant to be there at that moment just like the carnival. I stopped behind the wreck, kept my headlights on to illuminate the scene, threw the car into park and put the hazard lights on. I jumped out with no consideration of the relentless storm, ran to the window, and peered through it while pulling on the door handle. It wouldn't budge.

Even through my rain-soaked glasses and with only his profile showing I could tell it was him. I called to him, "Larry, can you hear me?" and after a moment, "Wake up, Larry you have to get out!"

As if on cue the front end exploded and with the hood still shielding most of the engine from the rain the fire raged beneath it. This time I didn't stand there and call out to him but, instead, ran toward the back of my mother's car. When I was halfway there, I heard it. The blood curdling scream that I knew was coming. I didn't miss a step. I got to the trunk and opened it, pulled out the extinguisher I had put there after that first time I dreamt of this night and ran back to my brother. I pulled the pin, inverted the extinguisher, and emptied it under the hood. The fire died and as I stepped to Larry's window. I heard my brother cry out, *please help me!*

"I'm here, and I'll get you out," I shouted.

He turned toward me and suddenly went quiet as a look of recognition came over his face. "Tiger eyes," and after a moment, "I'm so sorry." His words caused a wave of emotion to rise up in me, disorienting me, but only for a moment.

"Lean away, Larry, and turn your face. I'm going to break the window."

He turned and I raised the empty canister I still had in my hand and struck the window twice, the second time harder than the first. It shattered into a thousand harmless pieces. I dropped the canister, reached into the car, and began to brush the glass off my brother. It was only then that I could see how dire the situation was. There was a lot of blood coming from a gash in Larry's head and the steering wheel had him pinned back against the seat. I couldn't see his legs, but I was sure they would be pinned. With that amount of blood loss and the trauma I knew it was just a matter of time before he went into shock. There was precious little I could do. I picked up the empty canister once more and circled the car to the passenger's window. I tried the door even though it was obvious it would not open with the amount of damage it sustained.

After confirming the obvious I called out to Larry, "Shield your eyes, Larry."

His response was incoherent, and I could see he was running out of time. I used the canister again needing only one try this time. I cleared what glass remained in the frame and climbed through. Once in, I tore off a piece of my blouse and used it to put pressure on the head wound.

"Larry, listen to me. You have to stay with me. Do not go to sleep! Do you hear me, Larry?"

"It's OK, Shirley Mae. It's alright now."

"No, Larry, you've lost a lot of blood. You'll be okay but you have to stay awake and don't try to move."

"Don't you understand, Shirley Mae? It doesn't matter what happens to me. Your being here proves that."

I didn't understand but I thought it best to keep him talking so I asked, "What does it prove, Larry? I don't understand."

"Don't you see? It doesn't matter if I leave this place because I'll just start up again somewhere else like you did."

"I'm not sure it works that way, Larry." I answered truthfully then continued, "besides you have a life here with family and friends who love you. I don't think we get do overs whenever we want them."

"Then why did you? Why did you get this second life?"

"Why is the last mystery that will be revealed to us when it is time," I said. The words came to my mind from a memory of a previous life. Spoken to me when, like Larry, I asked the same question.

I could hear the ambulance siren somewhere from behind us and a minute later headlights started to pour light on us.

"The ambulance is coming, Larry. You're going to be alright. Listen to me closely, before they get here. I don't know how but our lives are somehow connected. You know this too. They have always been ever since I woke up and found myself starting this life at five years old but the stories you write are not about my life."

"How can you say that?" Larry protested.

"Please listen," I continued, "the universe is a strange place and none of us understand it, but there is one thing I have come to firmly believe. I don't believe you are writing stories about my life; I believe your stories are *creating* my life."

An expression of astonishment came over Larry's face as he struggled to fathom the full implication of what I just declared. He was quiet for a few moments looking down and then turned to look at me. Tears were flowing down his face, and he began to sob.

I took his hand and quietly said, "It's okay, big brother. It's all good now."

The ambulance drivers were at the door just as the rain stopped and I took my eyes off Larry for a moment.

"His legs are pinned, and he's lost a lot of blood." I yelled to the paramedic." Then I looked back. His eyes were closed.

"You'll be alright, pal. We're going to get you out." One of them reassured Larry but I could tell he had lost consciousness.

I was about to explain to him what happened when he started up a deafening circular saw and started cutting away the door. I kissed my brother on his cheek, and quickly got out of the way by climbing back out the passenger window. It took them only a few minutes to free him from the wreck and by the time I got back in my mother's car, found a place to turn around, and get back to the wreck, the ambulance had reached the top of the hill. The flashing lights disappeared but I knew where they were going so, I didn't hurry.

***

When I got to the Hospital, I went straight to the emergency room and asked if the ambulance carrying my brother had delivered him yet.

The nurse looked a little confused at the question, responding, "Are you sure they were bringing him here, ma'am?"

"Yes, I'm sure." I said.

"I'm sorry, but we are not expecting an ambulance in fact it's been a very slow night."

"But I called here about an hour ago for an ambulance. Are you saying it was dispatched from a different hospital?"

"Now I know you're mixed up, mam because I haven't left this desk for the last three hours and no one called here for an ambulance."

I was about to call her a liar explaining that I called from the pay phone directly across from her when the realization hit me. A smile slowly grew on my face as I looked at the confused nurse and said, "Never mind. It's all good now."

I slowly walked to the elevator, pushed the up button and as I waited, I opened my coat and saw my blouse was still missing the piece I had torn away. A feeling of peace came over me and somehow, I knew everything was as it should be. When I reached my mother's room she was sitting up and my Aunt Shirley was helping her eat. She told me that about an hour after I left my mother opened her eyes and said she was hungry. I wasn't surprised.

15

I never saw my big brother, Larry, ever again after that stormy night. The dreams also ended and through the years I was left to theorize dozens of possibilities to explain the events that culminated on my twentieth birthday. Was Larry somehow creating my life by his writings?

Perhaps *creating* is too strong a word. Controlling may be more accurate but it too does not fit precisely. There was a definite cause and effect, but which is the cause, and which is the effect? Did my intervention at the carnival that day cause a chain of events that led to Larry's spiraling downward after his fifteenth birthday? And did his negative attitude that resulted from the embarrassment, caused by that story about me and that day, somehow have a direct negative effect on my life? I felt like a blind man touching a few grains of sand and trying to picture the entire desert. I accepted that there were infinite possibilities but the one I chose to believe was this: I needed to be in that water as rescuers looked for little Shirley Mae. Perhaps it was because, being her only child, my mother needed me more than the large family that I left behind. Maybe I needed to be here when my father was killed and once more after my mother had her stroke. With each ripple in time the possibilities grow, leaving us hopelessly unable to fathom the truth.

In the end I found peace in the promise given to me that all questions will be answered someday with the final one being, "Why?"

16

I remember dreaming that my head was in a vice and a monkey grinder was turning the handle, tightening it while rhythmically striking me over my head with a little hammer. I woke up and they were both gone as well as the vice but not the excruciating pain that was shooting through my head. A monitor on my left was beeping matching the beat of the monkey's little hammer and had the same effect. A slight stream of sunlight slipping through an almost closed blackout curtain told me it was daytime, but not what day or where I was for that matter. The lights were dimmed but I could still see well enough to make out the I.V. pole at my bedside and its tube strapped to my left arm. When my eyes started to clear I could make out a door and despite it being closed I could still hear sounds of people walking past. I tried to call out and get one of them to come in, but my first attempt only resulted in a sound resembling a dying frog. I was about to try again when I spotted the call button taped to the side of the bed. I pushed it, lighting the little red light but that did not stop me from pushing it over and over like my life depended on it.

A giant merciless nurse burst into the room, flicked on the lights, and yelled in a voice one would use to hail a cab.

"You know sir, that button works just like an elevator button No matter how many times you push it, the elevator doesn't get there any faster."

I started to miss the monkey who in retrospect was the angel of mercy that this nurse was supposed to be. I found a semblance of my voice and was able to squeak out, "Sorry, my head, in pain, need drugs."

That seemed to soften her somewhat and as she picked up my wrist to check my heart rate, she replied with a voice two octaves lower, "I'll get you some painkillers but I don't have a cure for a hangover. If I did, I'd be a millionaire."

"You mean I'm not dying?" I replied, finding my voice finally.

"No, you'll live, though no fault of your own. The medics said you're the luckiest guy they've ever met."

"Lucky? You're kidding, right?"

She dropped my wrist and as she put her hand on my forehead presumably to check for fever, she said, "The way they told it you must have hit that guardrail doing a hundred. There was virtually nothing left of the front of your car and somehow the rain put a fire out before it got to you."

"No, you're wrong. Shirley Mae put the fire out." I corrected her, recalling everything now.

"Come again. Who put the fire out?"

"My sister, Shirley Mae."

"Well, that's not the way I heard it," she responded indifferently while heading for the door, "but hey maybe they told it to me wrong. I think the doctor will be sending you home after he has a look at you. He'll be in pretty soon. I'll let him know you're awake."

"Please don't forget the painkillers," I called to her as the door swung shut but it never showed up.

The doctor came in about an hour later and gave me a thorough one minute inspection. He too told me how lucky I was with a tone suggesting I wasn't worthy of it.

"How you managed to get barely a scratch except for a couple of bruised ribs and that cut on your forehead is truly amazing. And about that cut on your forehead, well it was just lucky you found that piece of cloth and were able to stay conscious long enough to keep pressure on it or you may have bled out."

"No, that's not how it was. My sister tore off a piece of her blouse and held it on the cut."

"Okay, son if you say so but the ambulance drivers reported that you were in the car alone when they got there. It's possible she left before they got there but that doesn't make much sense. It seems more likely to me, with a head wound like that and the amount of blood you lost, that you were imagining things. Anyways I think you can get dressed and go home. Is there anyone who can drive you?"

"Where's the cloth?" I asked, hoping for some fragment of evidence of the truth.

"What?"

"The piece of cloth you said I used to slow the bleeding."

"Well, I don't know. It probably was discarded as hazardous waste. It would have been incinerated by now. Why would you want such a morbid souvenir anyway?"

"I'll call a cab," I said, choosing to ignore his last question in favor of his first.

As I climbed out of the bed, I immediately confirmed the bruised ribs diagnosis. I walked to my clothes that were sitting on a chair in the corner and started dressing.

I was making slow painful progress in the tying of my shoes when my mom and dad came through the door. They had called around when I didn't show up last night with the hospital being their last call.

"Are you alright, Larry?" asked my dad as my mom hugged me gently. It was obvious that they both had been worried and scared for me and I felt bad for putting them through it.

"I'm alright. They told me I was really lucky. I got out of it with no permanent damage. It could have been a lot worse."

My mom stepped back and sensed something about me. There was a change in my attitude that came through and she saw it. I'm not sure but I think she recognized something in my countenance that told her I had had another experience like the day at the carnival.

"Shirley Mae?" was all she said and I nodded back to her.

Even my father could see the change but only said, "Let's go home, son."

***

Most of my siblings came over that evening to celebrate my birthday and to see me once more before I shipped out the next day. After the meal, cake and presents, I asked everyone to sit down and let me tell them a story. I saw no eye rolling and I heard no sighs. Everyone knew that there was a profound change in me and it was a welcome one. I told them the whole story of the night and what Shirley Mae had told me. How she believed that I wasn't just telling stories about her life but I was, instead, actually creating her life story. All of us spent the rest of the evening discussing this and what seemed to be an absurd notion at first became more possible and even desirable.

We all know that our actions in this life affect others like a pebble in a pond creating ripples outward. So, could it be possible that our thoughts have the same effect or possibly greater affect not being limited to the physical barriers as in the metaphorical pond? After all, countless studies have shown in varying degrees that there is power in positive thought and that the power of suggestion is very powerful and even the power of prayer has been shown to exhibit physical results in some cases. Is it such a great leap from there to believing that our thoughts and attitudes affect all that exists including other universes that have also been theorized by the great minds of our time.

In the end all these theories didn't matter to me because I know that my little sister, Shirley Mae, is alive and living another life that was necessary for her to live. We didn't want to lose her, and we were left asking the question, *why.*

Each time that question comes to my mind these days I remember Shirley Mae's words, "Why, is the last mystery that will be revealed to us when it is time."

ABOUT THE AUTHOR

I was born into a large working-class family. Although money was always in short supply, which resulted in hardship at times, my young life was also filled with wonderful family times and events. We learned to cherish each other, and together with my wife Sandy, this love of family was passed onto our own children, which we believe is our greatest gift to them. I made up stories for my children when they were young but never wrote anything down until they encouraged me to do so after they started their own families. I discovered not only the sheer joy of writing but also its cathartic effect.

For more titles by Larry George Pickett,
visit www.pandamoniumpublishing.com/shop
The Youngest Champion

Catrina is a courageous little girl who is relying on the bravery of her brothers to save her life! She needs a bone marrow transplant because she has Leukemia, and only her siblings can help her. A beautiful story that shows the power of family, love, and the strength of the human spirit.

The knight knelt down, crouching low until he was face to face with Trevor. His voice became softer as he said, "It is plain to see you love your sister very much. To offer all that you have, including your own life, takes a very special kind of courage."

Just as Prince Trevor was about to fall into the deepest sleep he had ever slept, he asked one last question. "But how will I know you have been victorious over Leuki?"

The last words he heard from the knight were, "You will see the answer in your sister's smile."

Written by Larry George Pickett, illustrated by Alex Goubar, 2021 Pandamonium Publishing House.

Order your copies on Amazon or visit your local bookstore for more titles by Pandamonium Publishing House.

Check out our virtual courses,
classes, and workshops by scanning
the code, or by visiting
www.pandamoniumpublishing.com